I WON'T SHARE!

No part of this publication may be reproduced, stored in a retrieval system, or transmitted in any form or by any means, electronic, mechanical, photocopying, recording, or otherwise, without written permission of the publisher. For information regarding permission, write to Scholastic Inc., Attention: Permissions Department, 557 Broadway, New York, NY 10012.

Library of Congress Cataloging-in-Publication Data is available.

ISBN 978-0-439-77353-9

12 11 10 9 8 7 6 5 4 3 2 1   10 11 12 13 14 15/0

Printed in the U.S.A. 40 • This edition first printing, May 2010

SCHOLASTIC READER
LEVEL **1**
50-250 WORDS

I WON'T SHARE!

by Hans Wilhelm

Cartwheel
·B·O·O·K·S·®

SCHOLASTIC INC.
New York Toronto London Auckland
Sydney Mexico City New Delhi Hong Kong

This is my toy Squeaky.

I love to play with Squeaky.

Let go!
It's *mine*!

Give me back my toy.

Wait!
That is *my* Squeaky.

Good!
He dropped it!

Grrrr...
I won't share!
Go away!

This is no fun.

I have an idea!

Hey!
Let's play catch!

Good catch, Buddy!

Get it, Scottie!

Now it's my turn.

I love this game.

Sharing is so much fun!